MW00879142

THE LIE

THE DO-OVER

THE LIE

GLASKO KLEIN

darbycreek
MINNEAPOLIS

Darby Creek
A division of Lerner Publishing Group, Inc.
241 First Avenue North
Minneapolis, MN 55401 USA

For reading levels and more information, look up this title at www.lernerbooks.com.

Image credits: Fabio Alcini/Shutterstock.com; VshenZ/Shutterstock.com.

Main body text set in Janson Text LT Std 12/17.5.
Typeface provided by Adobe Systems.

Library of Congress Cataloging-in-Publication Data

Names: Klein, Glasko, 1990– author.
Title: The lie / Glasko Klein.
Description: Minneapolis : Darby Creek, [2019] | Series: The do-over | Summary:
    High school freshman Leanna regrets giving bad advice to spare her friend Jenny's
    feelings, but given the opportunity for a do-over, will she make a better choice?
Identifiers: LCCN 2018023423 (print) | LCCN 2018030150 (ebook) |
    ISBN 9781541541955 (eb pdf) | ISBN 9781541540323 (lb : alk. paper) |
    ISBN 9781541545519 (pb : alk. paper)
Subjects: | CYAC: Tennis—Fiction. | Best friends—Fiction. | Friendship—Fiction. |
    High schools—Fiction. | Schools—Fiction.
Classification: LCC PZ7.1.K643 (ebook) | LCC PZ7.1.K643 Lie 2019 (print) | DDC
    [Fic]—dc23

LC record available a https://lccn.loc.gov/2018023423

Manufactured in the United States of America
1-45237-36619-9/17/2018

TO SONDY McLINN—
THANKS FOR THE LESSONS.

1

Since the summer between second and third grade, Leanna and Jenny's friendship lived and breathed on the tennis court. From the time the nets went up in spring to the first snow of the season, the two spent almost every afternoon hitting balls or relaxing on the courtside benches, chatting idly and waiting for the arrival of their next challengers.

Although they had both started playing at the same time, over the years Leanna grew into the much stronger player of the two. Still, this lopsided partnership hadn't affected their friendship. Besides, as soon as their gap in skill became too wide to ignore, the two simply adjusted their routine—Leanna covered the whole back of the court and Jenny covered the net.

By the time they were in seventh grade, the two got a reputation as the team to beat in the unofficial Tetterman's Pond doubles league. By eighth grade, resentful whispers had started to spread among the competition that Leanna was carrying the team. But Leanna ignored them. Jenny might not have been as fast on the court or as mean with her backhand, which was her weakest stroke, but Leanna loved playing with her best friend.

They were now almost two months into their second semester as high school freshmen, and spring had arrived early. On their way home from school the night before, Jenny and Leanna had swung by Tetterman's and saw that the nets had been set up early as well.

The next morning, Leanna had woken up feeling the familiar, electric thrill of the first day of the tennis season. As always, Leanna and Jenny headed straight to Tetterman's as soon as school let out, but this year Leanna was even more excited than usual. Playing at Tetterman's was great and all, but now that they were in high school, they could finally try out for the Kramer High girls' team. Any girl with a racquet could join the C-squad, but Leanna was determined to make the JV team. She had thought of little else all semester.

Jenny was a little bit less excited to be entering the big leagues. While they both loved the game equally, Jenny was worried that the gap between their skills would be even more obvious if they weren't on an actual team together—especially if she wound up on C-squad and Leanna made it onto JV, which seemed likely.

The air at the park was still thick with wetness from the recent snowmelt. Leanna and Jenny volleyed at the net, trying to get in a quick warm-up before any challengers turned up. It didn't take long for another pair of Tetterman's Pond regulars to arrive—the Gartner Twins, Kelsey and Teddy. The two looked almost identical, with athletic builds and long legs.

"Well, Ted, looks like we're not the only ones excited for the season to start this year," Kelsey said loudly, glancing in Leanna and Jenny's direction.

Unlike Kelsey, Teddy seemed to be genuinely happy to see them. "So we aren't! Great to see you both! Anyone up for a friendly match?" he beamed. Despite looking mostly alike, the twins couldn't be more different when it came to their attitudes. While Kelsey was cold and competitive, Teddy seemed to come down to the courts for the sole purpose of having a good time.

Jenny kept her concentration locked on the rally, but without missing a stroke Leanna called out to her across the net, "What was our record last year, Jen? Fifteen and four?"

Their pace was easy, but trying to talk and play at the same time made Jenny stumble. Almost interrupting their rally, she called back across the net, "Yep, fifteen four."

"And which team was it that managed to score some of those wins against the famous Leanna?" Kelsey called out as she approached their court. "Sorry, I mean *Jenny and Leanna*—sometimes it's easy to forget it's not a one-woman operation, even when you're both on the same side of the court."

Leanna shrugged off Kelsey's taunts, returning the next ball with an easy confidence, but Jenny whiffed on her next stroke, sending the ball straight into the net.

"If you were as good at playing tennis as you are at talking, maybe one of these years you'll need more than one hand to count your wins," Leanna shot back, strolling toward the edge of the court to meet their rivals with Jenny following slowly. "And to answer your question, Teddy, we would love to play a set or two."

"Perfect!" Teddy replied eagerly, sliding his racquet out of its bag and rolling his shoulders.

"Well, let's get on with it then," Kelsey snapped, trying to smile confidently.

Kelsey's confidence was short lived. After easily breaking Kelsey's serve in the first game, Leanna and Jenny carried the set 6–3. Jenny managed to find her groove and contribute to the victory, holding her own at the net and returning a few vicious shots Kelsey launched straight down the line. As the group met at the net for a post-game handshake, Kelsey muttered something under her breath.

"Sorry what was that?" Leanna asked.

Kelsey glared at the ground while she wiped the sweat from her brow. "I said, why don't we switch up the teams for once and see how things go?" Kelsey sneered.

Teddy and Jenny both said, "No," at the same time, looking at each other in surprise.

"Come on," Kelsey whined. "We always do the same match up and I'm getting sick of it. We don't even have to do a full set—we can just play a couple of games."

Leanna looked at Jenny and sighed, then asked, "What do you think, Jen?" Leanna wasn't the biggest fan of the idea, but she realized that if she wanted to make the JV team, she'd have to get used to playing with different partners. "Do you want to just do best out of three?"

Jenny forced a smile. "Sure, Leanna. No harm in trying something new."

2

Leanna was surprised by how much fun it was to play with a stronger partner—she'd been playing with only Jenny for as long as she could remember. Teddy was no star player, but she found that even though she didn't have the history with him that she had with Jenny, she was able to focus more on her own game and less on being ready to cover for her partner's errors. After easily beating Kelsey and Jenny in the first game, Leanna and Teddy managed to hold their own against Kelsey's serve in the second, setting up a break point showdown.

Kelsey missed her first serve, so Leanna stepped closer to the net as Kelsey hit a soft second serve. *Perfect*, Leanna thought. *I can set Jenny up with an easy shot—maybe it will give her some confidence.* As the ball sailed lazily through the sky and over Jenny's head, she fell back and set up for the shot. Jenny's form was so convincing, and Leanna grinned, anticipating a perfect overhead smash straight at Teddy's feet. It was set to be one of Jenny's shining moments of the match, and Leanna was excited to see her friend make the perfect shot.

But she didn't. At the last moment, her eyes dropped and her shoulders followed, sending her racquet slicing the air just below the ball, which bounced off the court behind her. Kelsey made a dash to try and recover it at the last second, but it was too late.

Leanna's heart sank as Teddy let out a triumphant whoop from the net before calling out, "Whoa, I thought you really had me there, Jen!"

"Come on, Jenny, seriously?" Kelsey groaned. "She practically handed it to you."

Jenny glared back at Kelsey, but didn't say a word.

"Hey, it's all right, Jen—sometimes the easy shots are the easiest to miss. Don't let it ruin your day. We both played well today," Leanna said as she approached the net.

"One of you did," Kelsey muttered as she shook Leanna's hand. "Come on, Ted. Let's get out of here," she said before heading toward the bike racks.

After the twins left, Jenny and Leanna sat down on the courtside benches. Jenny let out a long sigh but didn't say a word. She didn't have to. Leanna already understood how her friend was feeling.

"Seriously, Jen, it'll be fine. This is the first time we've played since last year," Leanna said, placing an arm on Jenny's shoulders.

"Yeah, Leanna, but I didn't see you missing any shots out there," Jenny said. "Besides, it's more than just missing that lob—I didn't miss it because I'm rusty, I missed it because right before I swung I realized you set it up on purpose. You don't always need to be babysitting me on the court, Leanna. I'm never gonna get any better if you're just handing me easy shots."

Leanna felt her cheeks turning bright red.

"I didn't, Jen, really," she said, but she didn't really sound like she meant it.

"It's okay, Leanna. I get what you were trying to do," Jenny said, letting out another long sigh.

Leanna placed a reassuring hand on her friend's shoulder. "Did you really mean it? About trying to get better? Does that mean that you're going to try out for the team with me?"

Jenny picked at the strings of her racquet. "I don't know, Leanna. I really like playing tennis with you, but it's just a game for me. The team seems like it's going to be really competitive, and I don't know if that's what I want."

"Aw come on, Jen, it wouldn't be the same without you. And how am I going to do well at the tryouts if you're not there? I don't know if you've noticed, but every time I'm playing my best you're on the court with me." Leanna gave Jenny's shoulder a squeeze. "That has to count for something, right?"

Jenny gave her a small smile. "That's because I'm always on the court when you're playing, period. But I know how important this is to you, Leanna," she said, her smile disappearing. "I don't want you to feel like I'm holding you back."

Jenny wasn't entirely wrong—it had occurred to Leanna that trying out for the team together would be a risk. Still, as confident as she was in her skills, she was still nervous for the tryouts, and it really would help to have her best friend by her side.

"No, what would really throw a wrench in things would be showing up to tryouts and having the closest person to a friend there be Kelsey Gartner," Leanna said, grinning.

"I just don't want to embarrass myself," Jenny said, "but if you really need me there—"

"I really do," Leanna said. "What was our record again?"

"Fifteen and four," Jenny replied, sliding her racquet into its bag.

"And that wasn't all me, you know," Leanna said, and she meant it. Still, if she were being honest, it wasn't exactly a 50-50 split either. More like 75-25, and they both knew it. Of course, she would never say anything like that aloud to anyone. Especially Jenny.

"Fine, Lee, I'll try out for the team with you," Jenny said, smiling again.

"You won't regret this, Jen." Leanna beamed.

3

"So, the big day is coming up," Leanna's mother said, shoveling a healthy portion of green beans onto her plate. "Are you starting to get nervous?"

Leanna pushed her food around her plate with her fork and stared at the wall of the dining room for a moment before shrugging her shoulders and grunting in response. She'd been feeling on edge ever since the match with the Gartner twins earlier that day. Leanna was glad that Jenny had decided to go through with tryouts too, but now she was feeling the pressure not just to get her own performance up, but to try and push Jenny as well. It didn't help that they only had one week. Her mother didn't help either.

"It's all right sweetie, I got butterflies before my first tryouts too. But I pushed through my nerves and made varsity," her mother said.

"Yeah, Mom, I know. Believe it or not you've actually told me this story before. Last week. Twice," Leanna responded with a sigh. "It's not as inspirational as you think."

Leanna had grown up on stories of her mother's high school and college successes on the tennis court. After topping the roster for all four years she was on the high school team, Leanna's mother had received a scholarship to a top university to play on their team. She had even briefly considered going pro, but then she got pregnant with Leanna in her junior year. Her mom may have given up on her own dreams of tennis stardom when Leanna was born, but that didn't stop her from giving up on her daughter's chances to make it to the big leagues—or at the very least a top tier college.

"Well, I'm just trying to be supportive, Lee. I know it can feel like a lot of pressure."

Leanna just nodded and kept playing with her food.

"You'll feel more confident when you get a better read on the competition," her mom continued. "You and Jenny have been hitting balls down at Tetterman's at every opportunity since you were little girls. You obviously have commitment to the game, and that's all you need to win."

Leanna set her fork down. "That's the thing, Mom, it's not just about me. Jenny is going to try out too."

"Oh?" her mother said, chewing thoughtfully before continuing, "Well, what does that have to do with you, sweetie?"

"It has to do with me because I'm going to feel horrible if Jenny winds up on C-squad and I make JV," Leanna said, glaring at her plate.

Her mother let out an easy laugh and said, "Well, you don't have any control over that. I'm sure Jenny understands."

"But I told her I'd help her work on her strokes," Leanna said, resuming playing with her food.

It was her mother's turn to sigh now. "Well, honey, I'm sure you'll do what you can, but at the end of the day you have to focus on yourself. When they're watching you at tryouts they're not going to be looking to see how well you coached your friend, they're going to be looking at what you have to offer the team."

"I know, Mom. I get it," Leanna said.

Her mother paused for a moment and began eating again. "I'm just trying to be realistic, and you should be too. I love that you love tennis, but I also love that you're good at it. I just want you to keep in mind the doors it can open for you, like it did for me—"

"Mom, really, this is not helping." Leanna was getting frustrated. Tennis had always been important to her mom, but ever since her dad left in middle school, their budget had been tight. Now that Leanna was in high school, her mom was already thinking about college, and she saw tennis as the only sure-fire way to make sure they could afford it. It was nice that her mom cared so much, but sometimes Leanna wished she would just let her focus on the problems she was having now instead of the ones she'd be having in three years.

"All I'm saying is that if it's going to be distracting, maybe you should find somebody else to practice with, at least until tryouts are over."

Leanna pushed her chair back across the kitchen floor with a loud scrape and stood up. "Are you even listening to what I'm telling you? I'm not just going to ditch my best friend so that I can get onto the stupid tennis team! You're impossible sometimes, you know that?" she shouted.

Her mother's mouth dropped open in surprise, but Leanna stormed off to her bedroom before she had the chance to respond.

4

"She really said that you should practice with someone else?" Jenny asked, bouncing a ball nervously against the court with the side of her racquet. "I mean, that's kind of harsh, don't you think?"

"Yeah, it is," Leanna said quietly, seeing the pain in her friend's eyes. She wished she hadn't brought it up, but Leanna also knew Jenny never would have stopped asking her what was wrong if she didn't tell her the truth. "I don't care what she says, though. I'm going to try and help you get on JV even if it means that neither of us do."

Jenny sliced toward the ground with her

racquet, brushing against the side of the ball and sending it spinning up into her waiting hand. She'd been practicing that trick for a while and had never quite been able to get it right, but today she hardly even cracked a smile when she managed to pull it off.

"Well, I don't want to be holding you back, Leanna," Jenny said. "I know you've always really wanted to be on the real team, and honestly I mostly just play tennis because it's something fun I can do with you. We both know you're the one with the talent for it. Besides, I wasn't so sure about trying out for the team anyway, remember?"

Leanna grinned at her friend in a way that she hoped looked reassuring instead of forced and said, "You're starting to sound like my mom. C'mon, Jen, you're a star when you want to be—you just have to stay focused and keep your head in the game. I know you're going to do great at tryouts."

Jenny beamed back and nodded eagerly, and Leanna couldn't help but feel bad. She really did believe that her friend would be able to get better, probably even good enough to make JV—if they had until next year to prepare. Less than a week really wasn't enough time to get Jenny into competitive shape. She made far too many small, technical errors to be consistent, and at the very least, JV players needed to be able to keep a competitive rally going. Still, she really did want Jenny to be there with her at the tryouts. They'd gone through every other major milestone together and a big part of her wasn't ready to let that go yet.

"Well, let's get to it then!" Jenny called, jogging to her usual side of the court. Her side just happened to be a little easier to defend because the sun was always at her back in the afternoons when they usually played.

Leanna forced another grin and reminded herself to stay supportive as she called across the net, "Sounds good, Jen, but let's switch it up this time. They're not going to go easy on us at tryouts, and I'm sure at least half the time the sun is going to be in your eyes. You may as well start getting used to it now."

Jenny fiddled with her racquet, and Leanna

caught a flash of concern on her friend's face, but it was gone a moment later.

"Fair enough," she said, and the two switched sides and struck up a relaxed volley. After a few strokes, Leanna increased the intensity and started focusing more on her placement, sending Jenny jogging back and forth between the alleys just to keep the ball in play. From the redness in her friend's face, it was clear that keeping up wasn't easy, but Jenny was able to hold her own surprisingly well. Leanna was already starting to feel a little better. *Maybe it wasn't selfish to pressure her into trying out after all. Maybe it was just the push Jenny needed*, Leanna thought.

"See, you're getting it now, Jen! We're just going to have to keep working over the next few days."

Jenny was out of breath but managed a nod in reply before rushing back across the court to return Leanna's perfectly placed shot. She made it to the next ball, but her technique had given out and she lost her grip on her racquet, sending the ball sailing straight into the net.

"Wow, Leanna, you're really good," Jenny panted as she retrieved the ball. "I mean, I knew you were good, but I'm actually starting to feel bad for all those kids we beat to a pulp over the years."

Leanna laughed. "Well, it takes two to strike up a solid rally—you weren't so bad out there yourself." They smiled at one another, but Jenny's grin quickly faded into another look of concern.

"What about the rest of them, though?" she asked.

"What do you mean?"

"The other girls. They all take private lessons and play indoors all winter and get new racquets every year. I haven't even gotten mine restrung yet," Jenny said, plucking nervously at the strings of her own racquet.

Leanna remembered what her mom had told her last night and said, "You can't worry about that. It doesn't take fancy tennis lessons and indoor court memberships and brand new racquets to get tennis skills. You just have to commit to the game." She sounded so much like her mom it surprised her, and for a brief moment she wished Jenny had been there at dinner last night so she could appreciate it.

"That sounds like a line from a sports movie," Jenny laughed.

"Well, there's a reason why they always have the same theme, right?" Leanna winked at her.

Just then, they heard the familiar skid of bike tires from the edge of the fence and looked over to see the Gartner twins pulling up. Jenny nervously spun her racquet in her hand, but Leanna saw an opportunity. *Teddy is good, but he isn't nearly as good as Kelsey. And even when he wins big, he's nice enough not to rub it in,* Leanna thought. *If Jenny can manage to even keep up with him enough for a set to be close, it will be huge for her confidence.*

"Hey," Leanna called out to the twins, "you two back for a rematch? The game is singles this time. I'll take on Kelsey."

The twins grinned at each other as they locked up their bikes. "You're on," Kelsey replied. "It can't hurt for you to get used to some humiliation before tryouts roll around, Leanna."

"You're right, I should get used to not laughing when you whiff the ball so I don't fall over and embarrass myself," Leanna teased.

As usual, Teddy either failed to pick up on the harsh edge of his sister's taunts or just chose to ignore them. "Sounds good to me! Let's get to it, Jen!"

Jenny squared her shoulders and did her best to look determined, but a trace of fear still managed to sneak its way onto her game face. "All righty, Teddy. I think I might surprise you this time."

And Jenny did surprise him. Just not in the way that she hoped.

5

Rather than the confidence booster Leanna had hoped it would be, Jenny's singles match with Teddy turned out to be a disaster. If she was being honest with herself, Leanna knew that she hadn't exactly done a whole lot to help things along.

She had managed to stay supportive of her friend during the first game—the first half of it anyway—but then she'd quickly got sucked into what was probably the most competitive match she'd ever played. She and Kelsey had gone point for point until Leanna had been able to secure the win. But based on what Teddy had told her, his game with Jenny hadn't gone nearly as well. Jenny managed to hold her own for the first game but lost her fighting spirit by the second. After that, she didn't win a single point. To make matters worse, Jenny had left the park without saying goodbye. Leanna had been so wrapped up in her game, she failed to notice.

Later on she had texted Jenny, who made up some excuse about having to get home in time for dinner. But Leanna could tell Jenny was upset based on her short, infrequent replies. So at school the next day, she had promised Jenny that they would hang out and do a non-tennis related activity that weekend to take her mind off of the match with Teddy. Jenny had agreed, although she had seemed a little reluctant. Leanna was starting to think encouraging Jenny to go to the tryouts had been a bad idea.

* * *

Now, it was Friday night and Leanna was waiting outside the mall, where they'd agreed to meet for some food court pizza and an early show at the Cineplex. Jenny was almost a half hour late, and she hadn't answered any of Leanna's texts.

Leanna let out a long sigh and checked her phone again, but nothing had changed since she'd last looked at it—not even the time.

She was about to try calling Jenny when she heard, "Hey, Lee!" Leanna quickly pocketed her phone and tried to look as if she hadn't been anxiously waiting.

"Hey, Jen, glad you could make it! Did you get lost and accidently wind up at Tetterman's?" Leanna said, regretting the joke as soon as she made it. But Jenny just smiled like nothing was wrong and gave her a hug.

"Sorry, I got wrapped up talking to my mom," she said.

"About what?" Leanna asked.

Jenny brushed a loose strand of hair out of her eyes and said, "Just tennis stuff, nothing big."

Leanna really wanted to ask her friend what she meant by that, but she bit her tongue, remembering how she'd promised Jenny a tennis-free evening.

Instead, she just said, "Let's eat!" and they made their way to the mall's food court.

Leanna was anxious to start the evening off on the right note, but it didn't take long for things to start getting tense. As soon as they sat down at one of the food court's tiny plastic tables, Jenny jerked her chin at Leanna's tray and said, "Going for the salad I see. That's a new one."

Leanna smiled nervously and did her best not to look at the greasy cup of breadsticks on her friend's tray across the table. "Well, I'm trying to eat a little healthier. Think of it as spring cleaning."

Although Leanna didn't go into more detail, she didn't have to. *Obviously she can tell my newfound taste for leafy greens is related to next week's tryouts*, Leanna thought.

Jenny tried to force a smile, but just wound up looking angry. "You know what, that's a good idea," she said, standing and picking up her tray. "I think I'll go trade up myself."

While Jenny was making her exchange with the cashier, Leanna tried to think of a way to change the subject. When Jenny returned to the table, she said quickly, "So what movie did you want to see? *Teen Witch 3: Witches in the City* just came out." It was the latest installment of a long-running series of movies about magically gifted high school girls, and the two had been fans of it practically since they'd first met.

"I dunno, I was thinking maybe we could try and sneak in to *College Party*," Jenny said, pushing her salad to the side of her tray and picking up a slice of pizza.

"Isn't that rated R?" Leanna asked.

"Well, yeah, that's why we'd sneak in. It's not like they're going to ID us once we're actually in the theater," Jenny responded before taking a large bite of pizza.

Leanna stirred a cup of dressing into her salad and frowned. It wasn't so much that she was afraid of getting in trouble for sneaking into a movie that was bothering her—she actually thought it was pretty dumb you had to be 17 to see an R-rated movie anyway. Instead it was that sneaking into a raunchy, fraternity-focused comedy was pretty out of character for Jenny.

"It just doesn't seem like your kind of movie," Leanna said, trying to be casual.

Jenny glared at Leanna. "What's that supposed to mean?"

"Nothing, it's just not what we usually do," Leanna said, trying not to get sucked into an argument.

"Well, we're big high school kids now, trying to get onto JV with Kelsey and all that. I'm sure *she'd* want to see *College Party*," Jenny said.

Leanna forced herself not to roll her eyes. "So this is about tennis still then," she said, cutting to the chase.

"Yeah, Leanna, it is," Jenny snapped. Suddenly she deflated and looked down at her food in embarrassment. "It's so easy for you, you know? You can just hop on the court with someone like Kelsey and all of a sudden you're practically a pro. It's not like that for me," Jenny said softly. "I know I'm just going to embarrass myself at the tryouts and then get stuck on the C-squad. I'm thinking of not even going."

It was the perfect way out for Leanna, but at the same time it was the last thing that she wanted to hear because it meant she had to make a choice. She could either continue encouraging Jenny and risk her friend being crushed if tryouts didn't go well, or she could let Jenny talk herself out of trying out for the team at all. But Leanna really didn't want to go to the tryouts by herself.

Leanna didn't doubt that she had the skills, but as tryouts approached, she was starting to realize how much pressure she was feeling. There was pressure from her mom, not only about following in her footsteps to tennis greatness, but also about being able to afford college. There was pressure to out-perform Kelsey—it was one thing to be the reigning champ at Tetterman's, but it would be even more satisfying to get a better spot on the team than her rival. There was even some pressure not to let Jenny down.

Leanna would have liked to think that

she was pushing Jenny to try out in order get her friend out of her comfort zone, but deep inside she knew that she was afraid to show up at tryouts by herself. She only had one shot to impress the coaches, and having Jenny there for support would make her feel more confident. *Anything I can do to make things easier is a chance I'm going to have to take*, Leanna thought. *Even if that means Jenny winds up bombing her own tryout.*

Knowing what she needed to do, Leanna took a deep breath and said, "Oh, stop it, Jenny, everybody has bad days. I'm sure you'll do great, and I'll be there with you, so even if it doesn't go well, you're not going to be alone. I promise."

"Really?" Jenny asked.

"Really," Leanna responded, cracking a smile and picking up her slice of pizza. "Now let's eat. And we can see whatever you want," she added.

Jenny grinned back at her. "Well you know it has to be TW3."

"I know," Leanna laughed. Thinking back

to all the times they'd watched the earlier Teen Witch movies made Leanna feel a little better about things. Their friendship had already made it through hundreds of tennis matches. Besides, she hadn't really done anything wrong—she'd just encouraged her friend to push herself. *Even if things don't go well, Jenny can't blame me for that, can she?*

6

When Leanna and Jenny arrived at the school courts for tryouts on Monday after school, the coaches split all the freshman into two groups, with Leanna and Kelsey in one and Jenny in the other. Leanna tried to keep an eye on how Jenny was doing and offer smiles of encouragement whenever the two caught each other's eye. She wasn't sure who the silent acknowledgements benefited more, her or Jenny—the competition was fiercer than she'd expected, and it was reassuring to see her friend out there with her, even if they weren't on the same court. When the tryouts progressed from basic drills to more competitive, head-to-head play, Leanna wound up facing off with Kelsey again.

"Nice to see how you do without that pal of yours," Kelsey sneered from the other side of the court. Leanna bent down to scoop up the ball she had just smacked straight into the net. Kelsey's first serve had been wicked.

Losing the first rally hurt, but Kelsey's words did even more damage. Leanna knew she had a point. She had been a bundle of nerves all day worrying that her encouragement hadn't been enough and that Jenny was going to back out of tryouts at the last second. She had been so relieved when she met Jenny at her locker after class and saw her pulling out her racquet. But Leanna brushed off the memory and tried to focus on the match. Kelsey was in rare form, and Leanna had to start playing on her level if she had any chance of making the team. *Okay, Leanna, concentrate*, she thought. *You can worry about Jenny later.*

"Hey, you ready over there?" Kelsey called out from the baseline, where she was anxiously bouncing a ball against the surface of the court. "You can think your deep thoughts later."

Leanna jogged back to her own baseline and called, "Let's see it then, Gartner. Hope you didn't tire yourself out too much with that first serve."

Kelsey hammered the ball straight into the inside corner of Leanna's service box, but this time Leanna was ready. With a perfect block, she sent the return deep into the court. She advanced toward the net, ready for Kelsey's next shot. When it came, Leanna crouched down and answered with a perfect drop shot that sent Kelsey charging toward the net too. Kelsey got there, but barely, and she popped up a weak return that Leanna easily swatted toward the back of the court where Kelsey had just been. *That's more like it*, Leanna thought. *Now I just have to do that a hundred more times and I have this in the bag.*

As Leanna slipped into the zone, she didn't just forget to shoot Jenny an encouraging glance now and then, she forgot she was there at all. It took all her energy just to keep up with Kelsey, who had found her own groove. By the end of the first three game mini-set, they were running each other ragged on every point, sprinting from one side of the court to the other to return each other's ground strokes then pressing up to the net for an equally punishing exchange of volleys.

Finally, after an intense showdown at the net for the set point, Leanna managed to clinch the first set by dropping the ball into the back court with a well-placed lob. Kelsey pivoted and dropped back with a sprint worthy of the Olympics, but it wasn't enough. She couldn't catch a piece of the ball.

"Wow, Kelsey, you got good. Like, really good," Leanna panted as they both grabbed their water bottles.

Kelsey wiped the sweat from her forehead with the back of her hand and smiled—and for once it seemed genuine. "Well," she replied between breaths, "we're in the big leagues now. Did you really think I was going to let you get a top spot without a fight?"

Kelsey managed to win the second set with

some tricky maneuvering of her own, pulling out a technique Leanna had never seen her use before—the kick serve. *She must have spent all winter at the indoor courts across town practicing that*, Leanna thought bitterly, wishing for the millionth time that she could afford to take lessons there. She made a note to keep an eye on Kelsey's serve in the third and final set.

The short sets made things easier in terms of endurance, but it also meant there was almost no room for error. Leanna had the serve in the first game, and she tapped into what was left of her energy to increase her aggression. She started rushing the net immediately, taking Kelsey's returns out of the air with vicious volleys.

Kelsey clawed her way back in the second game, taking advantage of Leanna's fading energy by keeping her running all over the court until she started losing her technique and accuracy.

Leanna's lungs burned and her legs ached, but it dawned on her that this had probably been the most exciting match she'd ever played.

"You really meant it about not letting me get a spot without a fight," she called. "Once we're on the team, we're gonna have to play together a lot more. The other schools won't even know what hit them." She could taste the sweat on her lips as she smiled across the court at Kelsey, who seemed to be having a lot of fun too.

"Yeah," she called back, "if they don't stick you on the C-squad once I'm done crushing you."

Leanna laughed and shook her head before jogging back to the baseline on her side of the court to start the third and final game. But going hard during the whole match made Leanna exhausted—her arms were burning, and she could hardly lift them above her head, much less keep her toss accurate. Kelsey was starting to wear down too, but that made their skills even at best, and it soon became clear that Kelsey had the edge. She kept up with her strategy of making Leanna run for every return, and it worked. Kelsey had fought her way to a break point when Leanna's arm finally gave out, ending the contest by sending her serve straight into the net twice in a row, losing on a double fault.

Defeated, Leanna dragged herself to the net to shake Kelsey's hand. "Don't tell anyone I said this to you, Lee, but you were on fire out there. Normally you're not half bad—of course, I'm a lot better—but you were really in the zone today," Kelsey said. "I think it rubbed off a bit on me too. We're going to rock JV this spring, just as long as you don't get any big ideas about who's going to be the star." She patted Leanna on the shoulder.

Leanna was too tired to care if Kelsey was being genuine or just trying to rub it in that she won. Instead, she placed her own hand on Kelsey's shoulder and gave it a friendly squeeze.

"You weren't half bad out there yourself. Why can't we always have that much fun?" Leanna asked.

Kelsey grinned, but there was a hard edge in her eyes that made Leanna feel a little uneasy. "Oh, this season is gonna be a blast, Lee. By the way, where's your little friend? You know, the one who's bad at tennis?"

Leanna winced. Here she was trying to make nice with Kelsey and she hadn't even bothered to go see how Jenny's tryouts had gone. Judging by the fact that she was nowhere to be seen, Leanna realized with a sinking feeling that it must not have gone well. She let out a heavy sigh and shoved her racquet into her bag, trying not to feel guilty for ignoring Jenny during tryouts. *But there's not much I could have done to help her anyway*, she tried to remind herself.

"I don't know, she must have left already," Leanna said. "I guess I should go find her."

As she biked to Jenny's house, she started feeling annoyed that Jenny hadn't stuck around to see how *her* tryouts had gone. When she arrived, she saw Jenny's bike out front, but when Leanna rang the doorbell, there was no answer. She rang the bell again, and when there was still no answer, she tried knocking. Finally, the door creaked open, but it was just Jenny's mom.

"Sorry, Leanna, she's uh . . . not here. Why don't you come back some other time?"

"Oh," Leanna said, glancing up the stairs behind Jenny's mom and seeing light coming from Jenny's bedroom. "I guess I'll come back tomorrow then."

Jenny's mom gave her a sad smile and gently shut the door while Leanna tried her best not to let this ruin the evening for her.

7

By the time Leanna got home, she could barely contain her anger. She was mad at Jenny for pretending not to be home when she stopped by, and she was mad at Jenny's mom for going along with it. She was mad at her own mom for constantly reminding her how much a tennis scholarship would help them afford college. Most of all, she was mad at herself for talking Jenny into going to the tryouts in the first place. Deep down she had known how this was going to go, she just hadn't wanted to step out of her comfort zone and do it on her own. Now she was mad at Jenny and Jenny was mad at her, and what should have been the best night of her high school career so far ended on a sour note. *If I had another chance*, she thought, *I bet things would turn out differently. Too bad life doesn't work that way.*

At dinner, Leanna tried to explain the situation to her mother, but she was much more interested in Leanna's performance than how things turned out with Jenny.

"But you said you did great, I just don't understand how you can be so down in the dumps about it," she repeated for the third time.

"Because Jenny didn't do well, and I kept telling her she'd do great, and now she's mad at me," Leanna said again.

But her mother wouldn't have any of it. "You don't have any control over Jenny's performance," her mom insisted. "I'm sure Jenny's just upset with herself and will be more understanding in the morning."

Leanna sighed and watched her mother cut the cake she had made to celebrate her tryouts. If she was being honest, her mother *did* have a point—Jenny was responsible for her own tryout, and it had been her choice to go. She couldn't be mad that she'd decided to try out and done badly. Still, Leanna didn't exactly feel like having a piece of cake and celebrating while she knew her friend was probably embarrassed and upset.

When her mother returned to the table carrying two plates of large slices of cake, Leanna said, "I'm sorry, Mom. I'm exhausted from tryouts and way too full to eat anything else. All I really want to do is go to bed."

"Okay, honey, I know how it can be," her mother sighed, trying to hide her disappointment. "I used to get so worn out after practice I could hardly even make it back to the dorms. You get some rest and we can celebrate tomorrow. After all, now that practice is going to start, you'll want to avoid going too heavy on the sweets."

Leanna just nodded weakly and headed to her room. She felt bad that she couldn't fully share in her mother's enthusiasm, but she really was exhausted. Sleep sounded like just the ticket.

She changed into an old T-shirt and pair of shorts and stretched out across her bed, allowing her aching muscles to sink into the sheets. But she couldn't quite manage to fall asleep. It didn't feel right to not at least try to talk things through with Jenny. After tossing and turning for almost half an hour, she decided to try calling her. *Even if she doesn't answer, at least she'll see that I called.*

Leanna grabbed her phone off the nightstand and dialed Jenny's number, but the call went straight to voicemail. After a letting out a frustrated sigh, she set her phone back down and pulled the blankets over her head. *Well*, she thought, *there's nothing else I can do about this right now. She's just going to have to get over it.* And with that, she drifted off into a troubled sleep.

* * *

The harsh buzzing of her phone jolted her awake. Dazed, Leanna reached an arm out from under the blankets to grab it, thinking it might be Jenny. As she rubbed the sleep from her eyes, she found that she had received several text messages from an unknown number.

They all said the same thing:

If you had the chance, would you do it
differently?

It wasn't like Jenny to try and get back at
her with creepy practical jokes. Leanna knew
that more often than not, angry Jenny meant
an absent Jenny, then after some time passed
Jenny would move on. The angry part never
lasted long, and it definitely never included
anything this confrontational and weird.
Jenny must be really *mad this time*, she thought,
worried and a little irritated herself.

Leanna brushed the hair out of her eyes
and sat up in bed, thinking about how to
respond. She briefly considered just ignoring it
but knew that wouldn't solve anything. Instead,
she decided to go with a straight up apology.

Jenny, I'm really sorry I pressured you into
trying out and things didn't go so well. I really
would do things differently. Did you block
my number?

Moments later, the phone vibrated again. Leanna pulled up the message.

Good to know. I guess we'll see.

Leanna wondered what the message meant, but she was far too tired to think about it any longer. *At least Jenny is talking to me again,* she thought as she returned her phone to the nightstand. When she settled back into bed this time, she dropped straight off to sleep.

8

The next day when she woke up, every muscle in Leanna's body was sore. But the pain practically disappeared as soon as she remembered how well she'd done at tryouts the night before. Then she remembered the she and Jenny were in a fight—a big, stupid fight that never would have happened if she'd just let Jenny make her own choice about tryouts. Leanna knew she'd have to figure things out with Jenny today, or it would ruin her whole week. *I'll start by figuring out if those weird text messages from last night had just been a dream or if they were actually from Jenny.*

She grabbed her phone off the nightstand

and began searching through it, but the messages were nowhere to be found. *Well, Jenny will come around*, she thought. In the meantime, she realized that she hadn't been very nice to her mother the night before. Tennis meant so much to her mom, and she had even gone to the trouble of making a cake. Leanna decided to make up for it over breakfast by making sure her mother knew just how excited she really was, and how much she appreciated all the support she had given her.

When she got to the kitchen, she immediately feared that things were worse than she thought. There was no sign of the cake on the counter. *Was Mom so upset that she threw it away?* Leanna wondered as she poured herself a bowl of cereal and sat down at the table. A few moments later, her mother emerged from the bathroom in her robe and made herself a cup of coffee.

"Good morning, sweetie," she said, taking a long sip from her steaming mug. "How are you today?"

Leanna decided to hold off on mentioning

the cake thing for now—she didn't want to upset her mother any more than she already had. Instead, she put on a big smile and hoped for the best.

"Great!" Leanna said. "I'm just so happy tennis is going so well. I'm sure I'm gonna make JV!"

Her mother pulled up a chair and sat down next to Leanna. "That's great, honey! I'm glad you're so excited," she said, smiling. "Just don't get too far ahead of yourself—you won't know for sure which team you're on until after tryouts on Monday."

Leanna's mouth dropped open in surprise. *Wait, what?* She slowly took another bite, confused. Her mother seized the opportunity to continue.

"And by the way, I think going to a movie with Jenny tonight is a great idea. I know you two had your fight about tennis last night, and I think it might be good for both of you to take a day off. You don't want to wear yourselves out, and you definitely don't want to risk getting injured out there. I swear they've been promising to resurface those courts at Tetterman's since you started playing there in elementary school."

Leanna swallowed her cereal with a gulp. *What is going on?*

"Uh, are you feeling all right, Mom?" she asked. She felt truly awful about refusing the cake, but that couldn't be causing this—was it a fever maybe?

"Yes, sweetie, I'm fine, although you're looking a little pale," her mother said, raising her eyebrows with concern. "Make sure you and Jenny aren't out at the movies too late tonight. You don't want to get sick this close to tryouts."

Leanna dropped her spoon with a clatter. As much as she didn't want to, she couldn't help but think back to the text messages from her dream. *Was that real? Did I make some kind of agreement with . . . something . . . without knowing it?*

She didn't want to trouble her mother any more than she already had, so she said, "Yeah, Mom, I'm fine. But I just realized that I didn't finish my math homework. I should get to school and see if I can get it done before class." Luckily, in all of last night's excitement, she really hadn't finished her homework, and for once that was a good thing. She was far too confused to come up with a convincing lie.

Leanna set her bowl in the sink, grabbed her backpack, and headed out the door. Whatever was going on, things were far from normal. She just hoped everything would start to make more sense once she got to school and talked to Jenny.

9

Leanna took a deep breath as she approached Jenny, who was standing in front of her locker and staring down at her phone. She had no idea what she wanted to say, but she also didn't know what she wanted to hear. If Jenny acted like nothing had happened and asked about the movie, it would mean that somehow Leanna had traveled back in time to the week before tryouts. But it also wouldn't be good if Jenny was still mad at her. Fighting with her friend was bad enough, but that would also mean something was seriously wrong with her mom, who seemed to think it was last week.

"Hey," Jenny said, glancing up as Leanna

reached her. Before Leanna could respond, she said, "Are you excited to hit the town tonight?"

So time travel it is, then. Leanna tried not to panic as a million questions raced through her mind: *Am I dreaming? How did this happen? Will I be stuck in this reality forever?*

Realizing she wasn't going to get answers anytime soon—if ever—she decided to just go with it. She took a few deep breaths to steady herself. "Uh, um, yeah!" she stammered. "Sorry I was just thinking about . . . math class." Leanna felt stupid for using the same lie with both her mother and her best friend.

"Sure you were," Jenny said, cracking a small smile. "Come on, Leanna, you know you don't have to lie to me."

Leanna felt the color drain for her cheeks. *Does Jenny somehow know?*

"I'm not lying, Jen," she said. "I've been having trouble with the proofs we're working on. Geometry is hard enough, and Mr. Kurr is so boring I can hardly stay awake during class so my notes are awful."

"Oh please, Leanna, I've seen your

notes—they're perfect. I know what's really bothering you," Jenny said.

Leanna's mind raced as she tried to come up with a response that wouldn't make her sound crazy. She knew that she had somehow traveled through time, and it was definitely bothering her, but how on earth could Jenny know?

"What?" That was all Leanna managed to come up with.

"It's the whole reason we're going to the mall instead of Tetterman's tonight—you told me what your mom said, remember? I know she puts a lot of pressure on you about the tennis thing because of her being a big deal on the college team, but you can't let it get to you," Jenny said.

Relief washed over her and she let out a forced laugh. "Yeah, you're right, Jenny. This whole tennis thing with my mom really has been bothering me. But we can talk about it later," Leanna said, before adding hurriedly, "or not. Totally up to you. If you just want to hang out at the mall and not even think about tennis, we can do that too." *It's not like it won't come up anyway*, she thought.

Jenny frowned for just a moment before she managed a tight smile. "Yeah, I don't know. I'll see how I'm feeling when we get there. In the meantime, try and think about what movie you want to see."

"Sure thing!" Leanna said, rushing off to math class. "I'll see you later!"

Well, she thought, *at least I have one thing going for me—I did all of today's lessons last week, so I can devote my full attention to figuring out how to stop Jenny from trying out. And how to make her think it's her idea.*

10

Leanna and Jenny met up outside the mall, just like they had the first time. And just like before, when they got their meals, Jenny went for the breadsticks and Leanna went for the salad. Leanna had spent all day trying to figure out the best way to approach the situation, but she realized that when it came down to it, she'd just have to wing it. She knew how things went last time, but she didn't know how Jenny would react if she did things differently and let her talk herself out of trying out. Despite not having a plan, she had decided to just bring it up and see what happened—she wasn't going to waste this perfect opportunity. If she didn't force the tennis issue tonight, it was bound to come up sooner rather than later, and after missing her chance that morning, she wanted to tackle the issue now.

"So I know we weren't going to talk about tennis . . ." Leanna started before either them even sat down.

"Yeah, and maybe that was a good idea," Jenny said, sliding into the plastic chair across from Leanna and grabbing a breadstick. "I mean, if it's really bugging you, we can talk about it, but can we figure out what movie to see first?"

Leanna had already seen this play out before, so she decided to try and get ahead of it. "Okay, let's see *College Party*." If she could throw Jenny off right away, it might be easier to have an honest conversation about tryouts, which was what they really needed right now. *Well, mostly honest anyway. I don't think I need to mention the time travel piece—she'll just think I'm crazy.*

Jenny stared back at her blankly for a moment before responding, "That's . . .

surprising. I was actually going to suggest the same thing, but I figured you wouldn't want to risk sneaking in to see a movie we're not even interested in."

"See, that's it right there, Jen. Why would we go through all that trouble just to see a movie neither of us actually wants to see?" Leanna said.

"What?" Jenny asked, setting down the breadstick as if she was preparing to have a deep conversation. "So hold on, you *don't* want to see the movie that you just suggested that we go see?"

"Do you?" Leanna asked.

Jenny tilted her head to the side thoughtfully before narrowing her eyes and letting out a deep sigh. "I mean, not really I guess, but—"

"So then why were you going to suggest it?" Leanna asked, cutting her off before she could finish her thought.

"I guess," Jenny started, then paused, trying to figure out the right words. "I guess it's kind of about the tennis thing. I know that tennis is our thing and why we're friends to begin with, but I feel like lately it's starting to come between us, which is weird. I really don't like that something we used to love doing together is turning into this weird problem. I guess I'm just not used to you being this super athlete girl."

It was Leanna's turn take a moment to come up with a response. "But we literally met on a tennis court. We've probably spent more time playing tennis with each other than doing pretty much anything else, other than going to the same school."

"Yeah, you're right," Jenny said, looking down at her plate. "But it's a game, you know? Like, we always play to win against the other kids at Tetterman's, but it's not like anybody is really keeping track of who's better than who."

Jenny sighed and cautiously looked up at Leanna. "Truthfully, this whole 'making the team' thing kind of takes all the fun out of it for me. I know you're going to do great, but if I don't make JV and you do, it's going to be really embarrassing. Plus you're going to start hanging out with all the girls on JV while I'm playing on the C-squad trying to be competitive in a game I don't really care about being all that competitive in. It sucks."

Things were going better than Leanna had hoped they would. *Maybe Jenny will talk herself out of trying out for the team all on her own*, Leanna thought. *If I give her a delicate push in the right direction, I can play on the JV team and save our friendship.*

"So what does *College Party* have to do with any of that?" Leanna asked, urging Jenny to continue.

Jenny bit into her pizza slice and chewed on it thoughtfully. "I guess I just figured that since this whole tennis team thing is kind of outside of my comfort zone, you'd understand how I felt a little more if I pushed you outside of yours. You know, it might show you—"

"But that's the problem, Jen. Why do you have to show me? Why couldn't you just tell me how you're feeling? I'm your best friend." While what she said was all true, Leanna suddenly felt bad about manipulating Jenny, even if she was just trying to save Jenny from embarrassing herself at tryouts. *But this will be for the best*, she reminded herself.

"You're right, it was stupid. I figured we'd end up going to see *Teen Witch 3* anyway. It's just hard for me to talk about this kind of stuff sometimes, you know? And think about what it's like for me—I keep feeling like I've been holding you back. I mean, that's even what your mom thinks," Jenny said.

Perfect, she thought, barely containing her relief. *Jenny's giving me an easy shot, and now all I have to do is put it away.*

Leanna wiped the pizza grease from her hands. "Well, I'm glad we're able to talk this out, Jen. So I guess you don't have to worry about trying out for the team anymore then."

Jenny's jaw dropped. "What are you talking about?"

11

Leanna immediately began to panic. Clearly she had misread the situation—or maybe they weren't quite as good at being honest with each other as she thought. Jenny's face was still frozen in a horrified mask, mouth open.

Leanna scrambled to come up with something to say. *Take a deep breath*, she thought to herself. *So the plan hit a bit of a snag. I can still recover. I shouldn't have expected something this delicate to go perfectly.* She decided to keep up the pressure, just like when she attacked the net as soon as an opponent started to struggle. She already knew how things turned out if she kept things to herself.

"Isn't that what you were saying?" she asked. "I mean, you were just telling me you felt like you were holding me back and that you didn't really want to play competitive tennis, so I just thought—"

Jenny's mouth snapped shut, her lips settling into a thin line that matched the creases forming on her forehead. "You thought what? That you wouldn't have to worry about me embarrassing you in front of the other girls if I didn't try out? Are you serious, Leanna? This entire week you've been encouraging me and telling me that you would help me get good enough to be on the team. But have you just been waiting for a way out this whole time?"

Leanna hadn't forgotten about the time travel thing, but she didn't think about how everybody else was living their lives at a normal rate, with no do-overs. It seemed like it had been forever since she had been trying to build Jenny's confidence, but to Jenny it had been less than twenty-four hours. Jenny wasn't reliving last Friday—to her this was just the

Friday after finding out that her best friend's mom didn't believe in her. Her best friend who was now telling her that she didn't believe in her either.

Leanna's heart dropped into her stomach. "Jenny, I didn't mean—"

Jenny pushed her tray toward the center of the table and stood up, her chair grinding across the plastic tiles with a painful creak as it slid back.

"This is unbelievable! I was just telling you about how nervous and uncomfortable I am about doing the tryouts that were your idea in the first place. And then you think this would be a great time to mention that you'd changed your mind about believing in me and would rather we just called the whole thing off? Seriously, I'm curious, Leanna—how could you ever think that was a good idea?" Jenny's voice continued to rise as she spoke, and she was starting to draw the attention of some of the other people in the food court.

"Jenny, please," Leanna begged. "I'm sorry. Look, why don't you just sit down, people are looking at us." As soon as the words passed her lips, she regretted them.

"What's wrong, Leanna? Am I embarrassing you in front of the food court? Do you think it would be better if I just went to the crappier mall across town so that you don't have to worry about looking bad in front of these strangers?" Jenny shouted. "Look, I'm out of here. Enjoy your salad—I'm sure the JV squad will be very impressed that you're trying so hard to stay fit for your Kramer High tennis debut."

Leanna sat in stunned silence as Jenny grabbed her bag, spun on her heel, and stormed off. *Well, that went horribly wrong,* Leanna thought, staring into her salad. She felt bad—terrible actually. Jenny did have a point. Leanna thought back to how irritated she'd been when Jenny disappeared after tryouts and then refused to see her, and realized that now Leanna was doing the exact same thing. She wasn't thinking about what it was like to be Jenny, she was just thinking about how *she* had wanted things to go.

Jenny was almost out of the food court by

the time Leanna snapped out of her thoughts. She could think about all of this later. Right now, she had to catch up with Jenny and try to make things right. Her friend was hurting—and this time it was definitely her fault. By trying to do the right thing and talk it through, she'd forgotten to do something else important—listening to what Jenny actually said. *If I would have thought less about what I wanted and more about how Jenny felt, I wouldn't have come off as so insensitive,* Leanna scolded herself.

"Hey, Jen, wait up!" she shouted. Racing through the mall, Leanna attracted even more stares, but she didn't care. She just kept shouting Jenny's name as she wove through the crowds, hoping Jenny would stop.

She caught up to Jenny at the bike racks, where she was rushing through putting her combination into the lock.

"Jenny, it's not like that," Leanna panted, trying to catch her breath. She placed a hand on Jenny's shoulder, but Jenny quickly shrugged it off.

When Jenny looked up at her, her face was starting to get red and tears were forming in the corners of her eyes, but it was clear that she was determined to fight them off.

"Actually, Leanna, I think that it is," Jenny said, her voice beginning to break. "You've clearly been lying to me all week, and it's obvious that getting onto JV is much more important to you than our friendship." Jenny seemed to regain her composure and she stood up straighter, faced Leanna, and spoke with more confidence. "I know you can't control whether or not I make JV. I know that I probably wouldn't make it anyway, but none of that matters. I just wanted you to remember that you're my friend too, not just my doubles partner, and at least try to be supportive, which I thought was what you were doing—until tonight."

Leanna wanted to tell Jenny everything. Maybe if she knew what had happened when Leanna tried to be supportive the first time around, Jenny would be a little more understanding. As much as she wanted to explain herself, she held back. There was no way Jenny would believe she was time traveling from the future and trying to save her from embarrassing herself at tryouts while Leanna got friendly with Kelsey and basked in the glory of her great tryout.

"I was just trying to keep you from getting hurt," Leanna said weakly.

Jenny snorted, then shook her head. "Well, you're doing a real great job, Leanna. Give yourself a pat on the back. But you don't have to worry about me embarrassing you at tryouts. Or ever again. We're not friends anymore. Goodbye."

Leanna hung her head in silence as Jenny rode off on her bike without another word.

◀◀

12

Leanna desperately wanted to make things right with Jenny before tryouts. She needed to make sure that Jenny wasn't serious about not being friends anymore, but Jenny didn't give her much of a chance. She wouldn't take Leanna's calls or reply to her texts, and whenever Leanna tried to stop by Jenny's house, she had conveniently just stepped out and her mother didn't know when she'd be back. For the next two miserable days, Leanna felt like she deserved it. She knew that she had been insensitive, and that her friend's feelings were really hurt. After all, if the roles were reversed, she would have felt crappy herself.

Still, tryouts were coming up fast. And as her mother had gotten into the habit of pointing out, she wouldn't get another chance at making the team until next year if she didn't play her best on the big day. Although the additional pressure didn't help her mood much, Leanna knew that her mother was right. She had already gotten one do-over, which was more than most people ever got. She couldn't count on getting another one.

Even though she knew she had to, it was tough to keep practicing through the weekend. Her mother wanted to help however she could, so they spent all of Saturday and Sunday at the school courts drilling and playing practice sets. It didn't help her feel any better about Jenny, but Leanna did notice that her game improved when she was playing against her mother, who was still a pretty exceptional player despite not playing as much as she used to.

By Sunday night, Leanna was physically and emotionally exhausted. She still hadn't been able to reach Jenny, and the matches she played with her mother were grueling. So when her mother encouraged her to take the night off to rest up for the big day, Leanna was far too tired to disagree.

"I know it's been hard with you and Jenny fighting and everything," her mother said over dinner, shoveling a second helping of pasta onto Leanna's plate. "But tomorrow you should just focus on playing hard and having fun. You've been great out there this weekend, even though you've been a little distracted. If you can keep your head in the game through tryouts, I know you're going to make JV."

Leanna sighed, mindlessly twirling some noodles around her fork. "We're not fighting, Mom, we fought. Now she won't even talk to me. I don't think we're friends anymore."

"Oh honey, that's nonsense," her mother said with a smile. "You two have been inseparable since elementary school. I know this fight seems like a huge deal to you right now, but as soon as the season is over Jenny will forget all about it, if not much sooner."

Leanna didn't want to wait until the season was over to make things right. She wanted to do it right now. She would have said that, but she knew her mother wouldn't understand. From her perspective, this was all just part of the plan she had laid out in her head. The plan where Leanna gets on JV as a freshman and is quickly recognized as a star. She'd make varsity, then get scouted by some top tier university, where her career would flourish while she got a free education and the ride of a lifetime.

"Well, I hope you're right, Mom," Leanna sighed, dropping her fork on the half-empty plate.

"I *am* right, honey," her mother said, giving her a reassuring smile. "Trust me—everything is going to be just fine. Everybody goes through this kind of thing at your age."

If only you knew, Leanna thought. High school drama and fights between best friends was one thing. But the pressure to make the right choices after she got a magical do-over? That was something completely different.

13

When Leanna woke up the next morning, she did her best to push her fight with Jenny out of her mind and stay focused on the matter at hand—dazzling the coaches with her skills on the court and winning a spot on the JV squad.

This turned out to be easier said than done.

At tryouts, she got off to a sluggish start. Despite her best efforts, she couldn't get her mind off the situation with Jenny, who was nowhere to be seen. Leanna held her own in the warm-up drills, but every time she fell into a solid rhythm, she made some technical error—too much wrist, not enough follow through, leaving her racquet face open—and embarrassed herself, which forced her to find her groove all over again.

She was starting to think she might wind up on the C-squad herself until she found herself facing off against Kelsey Gartner—again. That was when her competitive instinct took over. Just like last time, her and Kelsey seemed to feed off one another's energy, building up intense rallies that caught the eye of the coaches, who had appeared completely uninterested in Leanna up until that point. By the end of tryouts, Leanna was playing on a level she had only reached once before—during her first round of tryouts, before the do-over. Still, as she rode her bike home, she couldn't help but worry that her performance might not have been enough. Things had really picked up for her near the end, but after such a rocky start, the coaches might decide that she was too inconsistent to risk putting into a JV spot. She laughed bitterly to herself. After all of this, maybe Leanna had been right to pressure Jenny into going to tryouts the first time around. At least that way she wouldn't have been distracted by their fight and risked winding up on the C-squad.

Her mother didn't waste any time when Leanna got home. "So, how did it go, honey? I mean, I know you did great out there—you always do—but what do you think the coaches thought?"

Leanna dropped her bag by the door and went to the kitchen to get a glass of water, her mother following along behind her. "I did okay," she sighed. "Much better at the end than I did with the drills in the beginning. I don't know, last time I knew that I'd made it, but this time I'm not so sure."

"What do you mean 'last time?'" her mother asked, confused.

Crap, crap, crap! Leanna took a big gulp of water to buy herself some time. "I meant last night. I dreamed about the tryouts last night and I felt like I did really well, but now that tryouts are actually over I don't know how I did." She didn't like how easy it was becoming for her to lie. Leanna never really lied before, but now she felt like she was bending the truth somehow every time she said anything to anyone. *I guess telling the whole truth isn't really an option in this case, but still*, she thought.

Leanna's mother placed a hand on her shoulder and said, "Well, I'm sure you did great."

"Thanks, Mom," she said. "But I'm pretty worn out, so I think I'll shower up and then take a nap."

Her mother smiled. "Of course. And Lee, you should be proud of yourself for getting out there and giving it your all."

* * *

The shower was warm and refreshing, and as the sweat and grime from the court washed away, Leanna started to feel a little better about herself. She had done what she could, and that was something to be proud of. After she dried off and went to her room, it didn't take long for her thoughts to return to Jenny. Leanna decided to send her one last text, then leave it alone for a while. If Jenny still wasn't ready for her to apologize, she would just have to wait until she was.

Just got back from tryouts. I was really sorry to
not see you there. Also just want you to know
that I love you and I didn't mean to hurt your
feelings. We can talk when you're ready.

Exhaustion came over her in a sudden
wave, and it quickly became impossible for her
to keep her eyes open. She fell into a deep sleep
almost immediately.

14

Three weeks had passed since Leanna had last talked to Jenny, but life without her got a little easier every day. Soon she started to think her mother might have been right about their fight—that Jenny would stay mad all season. But Leanna also realized that this might not be such a bad thing. Both she and Kelsey made the JV team, but it didn't take long for the thrill to wear off and be replaced with focused determination. Most of the squad was older than her, and they had also been playing competitively for at least a year and were used to balancing their schoolwork with the rigorous practice schedule. Yet despite her inexperience, Leanna quickly rose up the JV ranks—but the higher she was ranked, the harder she had to fight to keep her spot on the lineup, which was always changing.

Kelsey found herself in the same situation. While she was clearly seen as a talent by the coaches, her spot was far from assured. She had managed to remain slightly ahead of Leanna for the first couple of weeks, but now the two traded spots on an almost daily basis. With the season now underway, there wasn't much time left before the first match, which the older girls told both of them usually cemented players into more permanent positions in the lineup. Skill mattered to the coaches, but what really mattered was performing well in actual match play.

"So, do you think you can keep it together against East?" Kelsey asked. She and Leanna were both packing up their things after a long afternoon of practice. In the past, Leanna would have thought Kelsey was just being snarky, but since they'd been spending so much time together at practice, it seemed like they might be shifting from rivals to friends, or at least friendly rivals.

"I think I'll be able to manage," Leanna said. "What about you? Are you getting worried about the rankings yet?"

Kelsey snorted. "Of course not. East is one of the worst teams in our conference."

Kelsey was right. It was pretty well known that the girls' team at East wasn't able to compete. Still, Leanna knew the first match was a huge opportunity to impress her coaches, and she didn't want to screw it up.

"Yeah, I know. I just wish that I had a nicer racquet," Leanna said. "This one is getting a bit worn out."

"Why don't you just buy one?" Kelsey asked.

Since she had joined the team, Leanna had started to fall in with the other girls, but there were some things about her life that they just didn't understand. Like money, and how not everyone had it. They knew her pretty well on the court, but they didn't know much about her personal life. They didn't know that her dad was gone, or that her success on the court meant a lot more to her family than bragging rights—that how she did over the next few seasons might determine whether or not she could afford to go to college.

"I'm saving up for a car," she said quickly. Leanna had also found that since she'd joined the team, lying had become a much bigger part of her life. It had started with the Jenny situation, but since then she had realized that life was easier when she didn't worry too much about telling the truth.

"Real ambitious there, Lee," Kelsey said, rolling her eyes. "With that job you don't have, I'm sure you'll have enough money in no time. But I don't want us to get embarrassed playing against East because you can't afford to shell out for proper gear. Normally I wouldn't do this, but what do you say to me picking up a racquet for you before the match? You can pay me back later."

Leanna felt her ears turn red. On the one hand, getting a new racquet was something she had wanted to do for at least a year. On the other hand, she knew Kelsey would never let her forget about it if she bought her a racquet. They'd definitely gotten closer, but not that close. Of course, Kelsey would also never let her forget it if she didn't manage to win her match against East, and Leanna didn't want to be blamed for a loss for any other reason than a legitimate lack of skill. She'd much rather get made fun of for playing poorly than for being poor.

"Wow, Kelsey, that's really generous," Leanna said. "Sure, I'd love to get a new racquet. Do you want to go pick it up together tomorrow after practice?"

"No, don't worry about it," Kelsey said. "I want it to be a surprise."

Leanna didn't like the way that Kelsey said "surprise," but she also didn't like having the shabbiest racquet on the team, and the next chance she'd get to replace hers wouldn't be until her birthday in July. *Besides*, she thought, *what could go wrong?*

"Okay, well just try to make sure that it's like this one, but you know, new," Leanna said. She couldn't help but think back to the time when it really didn't matter what sort of racquet she had or how well she did in a given match, back when she played tennis for fun. *Things change though*, she reminded herself, *and this is just one more part of that.* She just wished that not everything had to change. For the first time in a while, she found herself missing Jenny and how easy it was to meet at Tetterman's for a friendly pickup match.

15

The last person Leanna expected to see when she got home after practice the day before the first match was Jenny. But there she was, sitting in her living room and drinking iced tea with her mother.

"Leanna! Look who's here," her mother said, gesturing toward Jenny with her glass. "She said she wanted to come by and wish you luck before the big match against East! I thought she could join us for dinner!"

"Hey, Lee," Jenny said, doing her best to smile through the awkwardness. "It's been a long time."

Leanna wasn't sure what to think. She was

happy to have her friend back, if that's what was actually going on—but she couldn't help but be a little suspicious of her friend's sudden change of heart. She had started to get used to life without Jenny, and to have her sitting in her living room like nothing had happened now seemed strange. *What's going on?*

Dinner was surprisingly normal given that Leanna and Jenny hadn't spoken to each other in almost a month. They talked about school, the next *Teen Witch* movie, and even a little bit about tennis without anybody getting upset. After everyone had finished eating, Jenny suggested that the two of them go for a walk.

"Sorry things have been kind of weird between us," Leanna said as soon as they were out the door, rubbing her shoulder nervously. "I never meant for everything to get this messed up."

"It's okay," Jenny said. "I know you've been trying to apologize, I just wasn't ready to talk to you yet. I am now, though." She stopped abruptly and looked Leanna straight in the eye. "Look, Leanna, it's really great to see you again, but I didn't just come over here to catch up. There's something I wanted to talk to you about."

The evening was cool and the air was moist, as if it were about to rain, but suddenly Leanna felt uncomfortably hot. She had figured something like this was coming. *Is Jenny still mad? Will she apologize? Should I?* It was a conversation Leanna had been waiting for weeks to have, but now that it was about to happen, she suddenly wished she could put it off for just one more day. She wished things could just be normal, like nothing had ever happened, but she knew that was impossible.

"Yeah, I figured," Leanna said before trailing off for a moment. She took a deep breath and felt a lump start to form in her throat. Then she blurted out, "Look, Jenny, I'm really sorry. I know that I was a bad friend, but you have to understand that I didn't mean for things to turn out this way."

"That's not what I wanted to talk about, Lee," Jenny said. Her tone was a lot colder than Leanna would have expected after what she thought had been a heartfelt apology. "I'm still mad, but I have to tell you—Kelsey is not your friend. She's trying to sabotage you."

Leanna felt a chill run down her spine. The last thing she wanted to talk about right now was Kelsey. All she wanted to do was clear the air. "What do you mean?"

"I don't know, I just heard some of the other girls talking about it," Jenny said, then let out a heavy sigh. "I . . . I just thought you should know."

Leanna wanted to believe that her friend had her best interests at heart, but the timing was a little suspicious. "So all of a sudden you're really worried about how I do on the tennis team?" She asked. Some of the anger she'd felt when Jenny disappeared after tryouts the first time started to resurface.

"I just don't want you to get hurt," Jenny replied.

Leanna felt her cheeks start to redden. *If Jenny really didn't want me to get hurt, then why did she freeze me out for almost a month? Why didn't she try to understand the pressure I was under, and why didn't she try to see things from my point of view?*

"Really, Jenny? I'm surprised. I get that you're mad, but why are you trying to make things worse for me?" Leanna snapped. "Kelsey is actually pretty cool once you get to know her, and I don't think she would do anything to hurt the team's chances. She's even getting me a new racquet. Did you really think that you could just come over and have dinner then tell me not to trust my teammates and it would somehow make things better between us?"

"I'm just trying to help, Leanna," Jenny said, keeping her tone cold and even. "But if you don't want to listen to me, you don't have to. Just don't say I didn't warn you."

"Fine," Leanna said, "you warned me. But it's getting kind of late, Jen. I think I'm going to go home." She spun on her heel and headed back toward her house without looking back.

* * *

Leanna had trouble getting to sleep that night. Part of it was that she was nervous about her match against East, but the rest was because she simply couldn't understand why Jenny would try to make her distrust her teammates the day before her big match, especially when she was just starting to feel like she was part of the team.

I know Kelsey's competitive, but would she really try to sabotage me? And even if she wanted to, what could Kelsey possibly do to hurt my chances of doing well? Leanna did her best to push these questions from her mind and get some sleep, but it didn't come easily. The next morning she wasn't nearly as well rested as she would have liked to be, but the meet was going to happen whether she liked it or not.

16

The racquet Kelsey got for her was nicer than any racquet Leanna had ever owned. Still, it felt unfamiliar in her hands as she was warming up for the big match against East. She was exhausted from her lack of sleep the night before, and she couldn't get Jenny's warning off her mind. She still thought it was unlikely that Kelsey would actually try to sabotage her, especially given how generous she had been in giving her a new racquet. *Focus*, she thought. *Now is not the time to be worrying about Jenny drama. I have to keep my head in the game.*

Her opponent was tougher than she had anticipated. Despite East's poor reputation, the girl on the other side of the court had a wicked backhand and an even meaner serve. Still, Leanna managed to pull out a win in the first set by focusing on her fundamentals and making sure to conserve her energy. She didn't want a repeat of her matchup with Kelsey at the first tryouts.

In the second set, Leanna fell behind in the first couple of games but quickly regained ground in the next three, managing to outmaneuver her opponent by staying aggressive and charging the net. But each point was a battle, and she was starting to get tired. Her opponent was fast and had excellent placement, so even when Leanna kept up the pressure at the net, she found herself sprinting back and forth just to keep the rally going. She knew that if she was going to win her first match, she would have to knock the other girl out quickly before she started to get tired. *You've built up a solid rhythm, Leanna—now just keep it going.*

The girl from East waited until the sixth game of the second set to start pulling out all of her tricks, but thanks to playing against Kelsey, Leanna was ready for them. She had managed to fight her way to a set point through sheer force of will, and her opponent gave a last-ditch effort to break Leanna's momentum. Leanna recognized the windup of the kick serve immediately, so she pretended to put her racquet toward the center of the court as if she was tricked by the direction of the serve. Her opponent thought she had the point in the bag and dashed toward the net, trying to get a good position while Leanna was thrown off, but as soon as she left the baseline, Leanna dashed toward the outside, where she knew the serve would bounce.

When her opponent recognized that Leanna was onto her, it was too late. Leanna reached out and smashed the ball straight at her feet. Her opponent tried to recover, but her positioning was just too awkward, and she wasn't able to get her return over the net.

Now all that was left was to win the next two games and she'd win the match. *And I've got the serve*, she thought, smiling to herself.

She spun her racquet across her palm and bounced the ball against the court a couple times, making a mental note to thank Kelsey for using the kick serve against her in tryouts. Across the court, the girl from East was looking ragged and had a scowl on her face, clearly upset about how the last game ended. Leanna smiled to herself, tossed the ball in the air, wound up, and took a swing.

Pop! Pop! Pop!

Leanna looked down in horror. Half the strings on her brand new racquet had broken all at once.

She wasn't sure how she hadn't noticed before, but as she inspected her racquet more closely, she saw that the remaining strings had little grooves carved into them near the frame, as if someone had used a file to weaken them. The sneer on Kelsey's face two courts over was enough to tell Leanna what she already knew—Kelsey had messed with her strings on purpose.

Worse yet, she hadn't thought to bring her old racquet with her. Leanna's heart dropped into her stomach. *Jenny warned me about this,* she thought, mentally kicking herself. *I should never have doubted her.*

Borrowing another racquet would be easy enough, but at this point Leanna wasn't sure she could win her match anyway with so much on her mind. She felt awful for not believing Jenny and even worse knowing that one of her teammates—even if it was Kelsey—had betrayed her. As she walked over to the sidelines to borrow a racquet from one of her teammates, she considered forfeiting. That's when she saw Jenny standing in the crowd. Their eyes met, and suddenly Leanna's heart soared. *Jenny actually came to watch me play!* But then Leanna noticed something else. Jenny had her own tennis racquet slung over her shoulder.

"Jenny!" Leanna shouted, running toward her. "You were right about everything. I'm so sorry I didn't believe you."

"I'm sorry too, Lee," Jenny said. "I thought about what you said about Kelsey giving you a racquet and realized that must be what the other girls were talking about. I couldn't just leave you out here without a backup. Here." She held out her racquet with a smile and Leanna took it from her. The grip was worn down from the long hours Jenny had spent playing with her, and it felt good in Leanna's hands.

"Thanks, Jen," she said with a smile.

Jenny grinned back at her. "You've got a match to finish. Go get 'em, Lee."

Leanna jogged back to the court, where her opponent was waiting for her. Kelsey had tried to throw her off, but now Leanna was even more determined to bring home a win for Kramer. She took a fresh ball out of her skirt and bounced it off the court's surface, preparing to serve. With all eyes on her, she tossed the ball into the air. *This one's for you, Jen*, she thought. Jenny's racquet struck the ball clean, and she knew even before the ball had crossed the net that she had just fired off an ace. Everyone cheered, but one voice stood out from the rest—Jenny, her friend until the end, shouting, "Bring home the win!"

ABOUT THE AUTHOR

GLASKO KLEIN is a financial researcher who holds
an MFA in fiction from Long Island University
Brooklyn. He resides in New York City with his
fiancée and his bilingual cat, Umlaut.